My first book of...

Animal ABC & Numbers

Previously published as:
My First Book of Animal ABC
by Tiger Books International in 1989
My First Book of Numbers
by Tiger Books International in 1989

This edition published in 2010 by Chancellor Press,
an imprint of Octopus Publishing Group Ltd

An Hachette UK Company
www.hachette.co.uk

ISBN: 978-0-753720-46-2

A CIP catalogue record for this book is available from the British Library

Printed and bound in China

My first book of...

Animal ABC & Numbers

CHANCELLOR
PRESS

CONTENTS

A

B

C

A a

First in this Animal ABC
Is the Alligator down by the water, you see.
Though Monkey is safe on the letter A,
He'd feel much better if Alligator swam away.

B b

B is for the Bears, who can
    walk just like you,
Though you more often see them on
    four legs than two.
There are black bears and white bears,
    and some are born brown;
There's one in the picture who may
    tumble down.

C   c

C is for Camel, a beast
    with a hump;
He can move very gently or
    go bumpety-bump.
He lives in the desert, where
    water is rare;
If you saw what he drank at
    one time, you would stare!

D   d

D is for Donkey, a very
    special friend
Who walks on the sandy beach
    from end to end.
Johnny seems to be having a
    wonderful treat,
But I wonder how long he'll
    stay in his seat!

E   e

E is for Elephant, big,
  gentle, and wise,
With a very long trunk and
  very small eyes.
He knows what to do when
  little boys tease,
And soon helps them down from
  the tallest of trees.

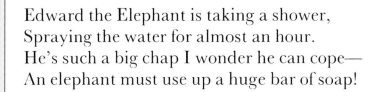

Edward the Elephant is taking a shower,
Spraying the water for almost an hour.
He's such a big chap I wonder he can cope—
An elephant must use up a huge bar of soap!

19

F f

F is for Fox, an animal sly,
As you surely can guess by
   the look in his eye.
I do hope the little birds
   perched on the letter
Will soon fly home where they'll
   feel much better.

G   g

G is for Goat, who can climb very high,
Scrambling up mountains as
   tall as the sky.
Perhaps he is frisky because
   it is spring,
So we can't really blame him for
   dancing the fling.

H h

H is for Hare, like a soft,
  furry bunny,
But with long pointed ears that
  look very funny.
In a jug Baby Hare is
  trying to hide,
But he's easy to spot
  with his ears left outside.

I i

I is for Ibex, a creature most shy,
Who lives on the mountains
   which soar to the sky.
He is pretty and graceful and
   quick on his toes
And has horns on his head
   wherever he goes.

J j

J is for Jerboa, who has a
   long tail.
If you try to catch him, you
   surely will fail.
He'll fold up his front feet
   and take a long hop,
And down to his underground
   hole he will pop.

K k

K is for Kittens with fur soft as silk;
They love to play, run around,
   and drink lots of milk.
They are useful to have about
   in the house,
And don't they look proud when one
   catches a mouse?

L l

L is for Leopard, well-known
   for his spots;
His eyes in the daytime are
   bright, narrow slots.
When he's prowling around
   in search of his prey,
Wise birds and beasts keep
   out of his way.

M   m

M is for Monkey; as all of you know,
Their tails help them balance
    wherever they go.
One of them has found a mirror
    and hat
And is now dressing up – just
    fancy that . . .

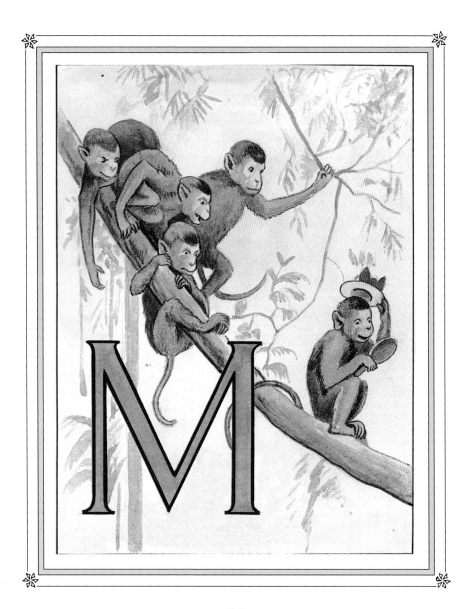

. . . but two of them are fighting—
see what they have found?
A bag, a comb, a letter that were
lying on the ground.
The party's not till Saturday in
the Monkeys' home.
There's time for all of them to dress
and even use the comb!

N   n

N is for the Narwhal, who lives
    among the ice
And is armed with a tusk that doesn't
    look very nice.
When he feels hungry, he swims
    through the sea,
See how he spears a fish
    for his tea!

O o

O is for the Otters, who live
   in our streams
And scare the poor fish from
   their happiest dreams.
They can swim very quickly and
   all like to play;
I do hope you get to meet
   one someday.

P   p

P is for the Porcupine
   covered with spines.
Before trying to pet him, you
   should ask if he minds.
When angry or worried he throws
   up his prickles,
But don't ever think that his
   coat just tickles!

Q q

Q is for the Quail, a very
    fine bird,
Whose call in the woods you all
    will have heard.
Look how Johnny the farmer hides
    by the tree,
Counting quail in the grass – one,
    two, and three.

R r

R is for Reindeer, much loved
   by the Lapps
(And also by Santa Claus,
   the dearest of chaps).
The reindeer is speedy and
   wonderfully strong
And jingles his bells as he
   gallops along.

Each Christmas, the Reindeer pull dear
Santa's sleigh,
Delivering presents here and far away.
To the roof of each house Santa Claus
springs,
And the children delight in the toys
that he brings.

S s

S is for the Squirrels, who
    live in the trees
And swing from the branches with
    the greatest of ease.
Nuts and acorns they hide
    in the ground,
So they will have food when
    winter comes round.

T t

T is for Tiger with teeth
   sharp as glass.
The stripes on his coat help
   him hide in tall grass.
But now he is hungry, his mouth
   is open wide;
I hope Monkey and his concertina
   don't fall inside!

U u

U is for Umbrella Bird with his
  feathery crest
And a set of plumage that sprouts
  on his breast.
He is a kind of crow and
  a little bit vain,
And I don't think he'd help out much
  in the rain!

V v

V is clearly meant for the Voles,
Water rats who live by the river in holes.
When they want to travel to visit with friends,
They ride on a leaf till their journey ends.

W w

W is for Wolf, a ravenous beast,
Always sniffing around in search
   of a feast.
He is easily scared by a very
   bright light;
Then you can feel safe for the
   night.

X x

X is a creature you've not
   met before
And you won't see again, for its
   days are quite o'er.
It roamed over the world when
   people were few;
It's a pity that one wasn't
   saved for the Zoo.

AN **X**E~X~-TINCT ANIMAL

Y y

Y is for the Yak who lives
    in Tibet,
Where very few visitors have
    set foot as yet.
He's covered all over with
    long shaggy hair,
Which helps keep him warm when
    there's snow in the air.

Z z

Z is for Zebra with stripes
   white and black
All over his head, his feet and
   his back.
Of course you know also that Z
   stands for Zoo—
A place for all the animals to
   look at me and you!

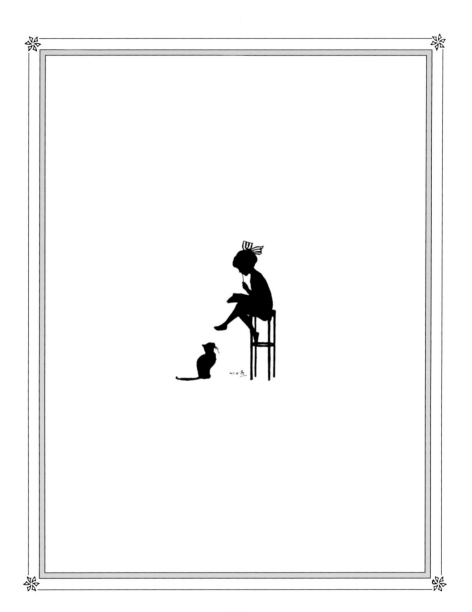

NUMBERS

"ONE"

"It's not much fun being on your own,"
Said Edward the elephant, all alone.
"I've got one trunk to help me eat
And one kind keeper to keep me neat,
But I would like some friends and
a bit of noise."
So he went to the circus, and the girls
and boys
Lined up to see Edward one by one,
And each gave the elephant just one bun!

"TWO"

Two by two, two by two,
The clowns and the zebras play.
Said a clown to a pair of zebras,
"We'll play such games today!
If you give us rides, dear zebras,
Such merriment we can share,
For a clown and a stripy zebra
Make the happiest kind of pair."

"THREE"

Look at the children enjoying the view
From the back of the camel who lives
in the zoo.
How many children can Mr. Jones see?
Susie and Sarah and Simon make three,
Bouncing about and enjoying the walk.
But what would the camel say if
he could talk?
"If Susie and Sarah and Simon make three,
I've still got one space on my back
that is free!"

How many children can you see in the
picture?

"FOUR"

The first parrot said
Through his shiny beak,
"Parrots can talk;
Parrots can speak."
The second parrot said
With his loudest squawk,
"Parrots can speak;
Parrots can talk."
The third parrot said,
As he sat on his swing,
"Parrots can fly;
Parrots can sing."
The fourth parrot said,
As he looked away,
"I'm not doing anything at all today!"

"FIVE"

Five penguins are diving in a pool,
Plunging through the waters cool,
Trying hard to catch five fish
To make a tasty dinner dish.

There are five penguins in the picture,
but how many fish can you count?

"SIX"

Sally was feeding six squirrels
With some nuts and some leftover cheese;
And the squirrels thought, "This
is much nicer
Than the food that we find in the trees."

They liked to go out in half-dozens,
Meeting people and playing their tricks;
And when they got home in the evening,
They would say, "Oh, what fun to be six!"

"SEVEN"

Let's swing a skipping rope;
Let's sing a song,
Counting or skipping steps
As we go along.

One, two, three, four, five, six, seven;
All good children go to heaven.
Seven, six, five, four, three, two, one;
We've hardly started; we've only just begun.

One skip, two skip, three skip, four;
Let's skip again; let's skip some more.
Five skip, six skip, seven skip, wait!
Seven skippers are enough, so don't be late!

How many people can you see
watching the skipping?

"EIGHT"

Bubbles here, bubbles there,
Bubbles blowing everywhere,
Round and shiny, floating free,
Some for you and some for me.
Can you count them? There were some
Which landed on my sister's thumb
And disappeared – I don't know where –
To leave eight bubbles in the air.

How many pipes are the children using
to blow bubbles?

"NINE"

Nine little monkeys
Playing on ropes,
The shy little monkey
Had high hopes
Of joining his friends
On the ropes below;
The other monkeys shouted,
"Get set, go!"
Now all the little monkeys
Happily entwine,
Eight plus the shy one
Making nine.

"TEN"

The pelican pool is always busy.
Pelicans like to drink and swim,
Pelicans like to splash and chatter,
Pelicans fat and pelicans trim.
Each day one more pelican comes here,
Pelican cocks and pelican hens,
Pelicans one, two, three, four, five,
Pelicans six, seven, eight, nine, ten!

How many pelicans are drinking?

"ELEVEN"

Seven plus four is eleven,
And twelve minus one is the same.
Eleven's the ideal number
For leapfrog, a wonderful game.

Four people squat down and play froggy,
The others jump over their friends,
Then squat down themselves to be
leapfrogged,
And that way the game never ends!

"TWELVE"

"Twelve passengers? Don't make me laugh!"
Said Geraldine, the tall giraffe.
"It's hard to move with eight or nine
And, oh, that poor old back of mine!
Not even Alf, my tallest cousin,
Takes as many as a dozen;
So please don't ever ask me whether
I can carry twelve together."

How many passengers *can* Geraldine carry?
How many children get left behind?

"THIRTEEN"

Thirteen birds upon the beach,
"Unlucky number!" hear them screech.
But Rachel, who is always plucky,
Thinks thirteen is rather lucky.
"You birds are fed; the sea is blue;
That's luck for me and luck for you."
Now hear the birds begin to cluck,
"We've all been fed, what luck, what luck!"

"FOURTEEN"

Fourteen balloons of different hue,
And sister Sally buys just two,
So twelve remain; then brother Benny
Buys one more, which leaves – how many?

"FIFTEEN"

How many children have snowballs?
How many children have not?
Some of the children are throwing just one,
But one boy has gathered a lot.

When you have looked at the picture,
And have seen all there is to be seen,
Count up all the children you see there.
The answer? I think it's fifteen.

"SIXTEEN"

We're playing wheelbarrows;
You can do the same.
All you need are arms and legs
To play this game.

Don't worry if you fall;
You won't come to harm.
Count as you go along,
Every leg and arm.

Eight arms, eight legs,
See them in the scene?
Add them all together,
And you've got sixteen.

"SEVENTEEN"

When I do my puzzle,
I first drop all the pieces
And count them one by one,
The number soon increases.
There should be seventeen,
And then I know I'm ready
To make the pieces fit
With hands and eyes so steady.

"EIGHTEEN"

What happens when you do the washing?
Soap and water go splish-sploshing.
Wring the clothes out – mind your legs!
Each garment needs a pair of pegs;
So when you hang up item nine,
You've eighteen pegs upon the line.

"NINETEEN"

I drew nineteen cats today
With nineteen tails and nineteen faces;
Instead of going out to play,
I drew cats in nineteen places.

I drew nineteen cats today.
I could have drawn a nice round twenty,
But I met a friendly stray
Who told me nineteen cats were plenty!

"TWENTY"

When Humpty Dumpty had his fall,
The king's men tried to save him.
So twenty soldiers came to call,
And this is what they gave him:

Twenty pills to make him better,
Twenty tubes of strongest glue,
Twenty get-well cards and letters,
Twenty bowls of steaming stew.

But all the pills and glue and letters
Brought by twenty soldier men
Couldn't make poor Humpty better,
Couldn't make him well again.

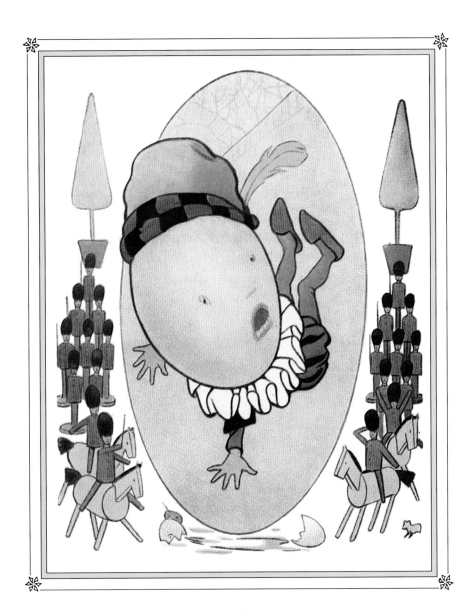

"THREE BLIND MICE"

Three blind mice,
Three blind mice,
See how they run!
See how they run!
They all ran after the farmer's wife,
Who cut off their tails with a carving knife.
Did you ever see such a sight in your life
As three blind mice?

How many buttons does each mouse
have on his coat? How many buttons
are there in the picture?

"SING A SONG OF SIXPENCE"

Sing a sixpence,
A pocketful of rye,
Four and twenty blackbirds
Baked in a pie.
When the pie was opened,
The birds began to sing;
Now wasn't that a dainty dish
To set before the king?

There are twenty-four blackbirds in the pie,
but how many can you *see*?

"SHOPPING"

"Hello, Mr. Grocer, please will you tell me
What you have here in your shop to sell me?"
"Butter and sugar and honey and tea,
Potatoes and coffee and bread," says he.

How many things does the shopkeeper
say he has to sell? How many can you see?

"TRAIN"

Four on the train, riding with glee;
Dolly got off, and then there were three.
Three on the train – whistle, choo, choo!
Baby got off, and then there were two.
Two on the train, having such fun;
Brother got off, and then there was one.

Who was the last person on the train?

"MARY, MARY"

Mary, Mary, quite contrary,
How does your garden grow?
"With silver bells and cockle shells
And pretty maids all in a row."

Can you count the shells in Mary's garden?

"SEA LIONS"

Riding on the sea lions,
Splashing through the spray,
Happy that the sea lions
Are coming out to play.

Riding through the water
With the sea lion pack,
So happy to be riding,
We're never coming back!

How many sea lions can you see?
How many riders?

"MRS. KANGAROO"

"Good morning, Mrs. Kangaroo,
I see you've brought your baby too."
"Oh yes, and if I hop or crouch,
My baby's safe inside my pouch."

Can you count the kangaroos
hopping across the bottom of
the picture?

"MONKEYS"

The monkeys make their way to school,
But not upon a horse or mule.
They do not take the bus or train,
They let their keeper take the strain.
He carries four to school with ease
But leaves one monkey in the trees.

"FLAMINGOS"

Great long legs and a stretching neck,
Both help the flamingo take a peck.
Bobbing his tail while taking a dive
Is the only way that a duck can thrive,
"Which is why," said a duck to his
brother Jim,
"Flamingos can stand, but ducks
must swim!"

How many ducks can you see?
How many flamingos?

How many cats at the bottom
of the page?

"CRICKET"

Do you know the game of cricket?
It's played upon a grassy wicket.
How to take the score to one?
Bat the ball and take a run.
How to take the runs to four?
Bat again and score three more.
Runs are scored along the wicket –
Now you know the game of cricket.

M.W.T.